MARLY

and the

Pre-Monday Blues

SHAUNTE HESTER HOBGOOD

ISBN 978-1-64471-752-3 (Paperback)
ISBN 978-1-64471-753-0 (Digital)

Covenant Books, Inc.
11661 Hwy 707
Murrells Inlet, SC 29576
www.covenantbooks.com

To my daughter, Shania Marie, no dream is unachievable. Always reach for the stars and beyond.

"I can do all things through him who strengthens me." Philippians 4:13

Love you forever and always.

It was Sunday evening, and Marie was watching her favorite cartoon while her mom finished cleaning the kitchen.

"All right, little girl, time to take your bath," her mom said as she walked into the living room.

"Ah man! Can I watch one more cartoon? Pleeease?" Marie asked.

"No, ma'am," her mom answered. "It's time to take your bath and get ready for school tomorrow."

Marie slid off the couch lazily, put her chin to her chest, and walked slowly to the stairs where her mom was waiting. She glanced up at her mom with hopes that she would allow her to watch one more cartoon before taking a bath.

"One…two…three…," yelled her mom as she began to run up the stairs. When she looked back she noticed that Marie wasn't participating in their usual stair race.

She walked down the stairs, sat on the bottom step and patted the empty space beside her. "What's wrong with Mommy's baby?" her mom asked puzzled.

"I don't want to go to school tomorrow." Marie pouted. "I really wish we could have these many days out of school instead of only two," Marie said as she held up ten fingers.

"I know, honey," her mom said reassuringly. "But let's be thankful for the two days that we do get." She said as she pulled Marie close. She stood up, extended her hand out to Marie, and they walked up the stairs together.

After bath time, Marie's mom noticed that she still appeared to be bothered.

"Uh-oh!" her mom said worriedly. "*Daddy*! We have a problem," yelled Marie's mom.

Marie's dad came into her bedroom and lay beside her. "What's the matter?" he asked as he noticed the sad faces in the room.

"I believe Marie has a case of the pre-Monday blues," Marie's mom said as she winked at Daddy.

"Oh my! This is serious," he said as he began to sit up.

"Daddy, I don't want to go to school tomorrow," Marie said as she crawled into his lap and looked at him with sad eyes.

"Can I tell you a secret?" her dad asked.

"Sure!" Marie answered as she brought her ear close to his face.

"I don't want to go to work tomorrow," he whispered. "But sometimes in life, we have to go places we may not want to go or do things that we may not want to do. But luckily for you, school can be fun. You get to learn new things, play with your friends, and, most importantly, you get to take a nap." He laughed. "Also, once Monday gets here, that's one day closer to the weekend."

Marie smiled as she rested her head against his chest.

*   *   *   *   *

"Rise and shine, sweetheart," Marie's mom said as she walked into her room. As she got closer to the bed, she noticed that Marie was laying there with a big smile on her face. "Someone appears to be happy this morning," her mom acknowledged as she planted a morning kiss on Marie's cheek.

"I am happy, Mommy," Marie responded. "I'm happy that it's Monday and one day closer to the weekend. But!" she yelled as she pointed her finger toward the ceiling. "Ten days out of school would still be nice." She and her mom began to laugh.

About the Author

Growing up as an only child, Shaunte Hester Hobgood had a very elaborate imagination, which she gives credit for helping develop her gift of writing. She is a graduate of North Carolina Agricultural and Technical State University with a degree in journalism and mass communications. Having a passion for writing, she decided to pursue her dream of becoming a published author. Shaunte is an avid music lover that also enjoys traveling and reading. She resides in North Carolina with her husband, Jerrod, and her daughter, Shania.